A NUMBER OF
ANIMALS

A NUMBER OF ANIMALS

CHRISTOPHER WORMELL

JONATHAN CAPE
LONDON

First published 1994

1 3 5 7 9 10 8 6 4 2

Text © Kate Green 1994
Illustrations © Christopher Wormell 1994

Kate Green and Christopher Wormell have asserted their right
under the Copyright, Designs and Patents Act, 1988 to be
identified as the author and illustrator of this work

This edition first published in the United Kingdom in 1994 by
Jonathan Cape Limited
Random House, 20 Vauxhall Bridge Road, London SW1V 2SA
in association with Creative Education Inc.,
123 South Broad Street, Mankato, Minnesota 56001 USA

A CIP catalogue record for this book
is available from the British Library

ISBN 0 224 04111 8

Printed in Italy

C7067388 99

CVB/15/C

For Daisy

I

Chick

One little chick, lost and alone.

2
Horses

Two huge horses back by the stable.
"Have you seen my mother?"
"Not today," the horses neigh.

3
Cows

Three slow cows sunning in the meadow.

"Have *you* seen my mother?"

But all they do is moo.

4
Turkeys

Four fat turkeys ruffling their feathers.
"Gobble, gobble!" they gab
and strut through the straw.

5
Goats

Five shaggy goats grazing in the field.
Their beards are hairy. Their horns are sharp.
"Baa-aa," they bleat. "No hens here!"

6
Geese

Six white geese waddling toward the water.

The little chick comes too close.

Look out!

7
Sheep

Seven sleepy sheep, woolly and warm.
The world is too big when you're all alone.

8
Ducks

Eight splashing ducks calling quack, quack, quack.

The chick cheeps to them,

but the ducks don't quack back.

Pigs

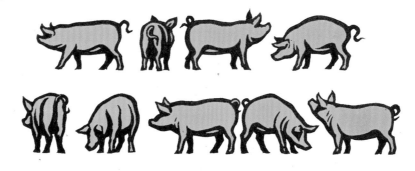

Nine pudgy pigs flopped in the mud.
"Wake up!" peeps the chick–
but what does he hear?

10
Chicks

It's his sisters chirping and his brothers cheeping!

Now there are ten chicks...

...and one mother hen!
"Here you are!" the little chick squeaks
and all ten follow her home.

1 2 3 4 5

6 7 8 9 10